# LINDA LEWIS'S

# WRITING GUIDES

## NO. 2

## WHY SHORT STORIES ARE REJECTED

ISBN 978–1–4709–7959–1

**Other titles also available**

**TWISTING THE NIGHT AWAY**

A selection of stories with twist endings

**LOVE IS ALL AROUND**

A collection of stories with romance as the theme

**CRIME SHORTS**

Stories featuring various crimes

## NON FICTION

**A MOTHER'S LOVE:**
**HOW I LEARNED TO LIVE WITHOUT IT**

**A WRITER'S GLOSSARY**

The first in a series of writing guides

A light hearted A – Z of terms

**WRITING FILLERS: HOW TO EARN £10 IN TEN MINUTES**

The third in the series explains how to make money writing fillers for magazines.

## INTRODUCTION

Rejection is horrible.

It doesn't help that, more often than not, we don't find out why our stories have been sent back.

When it comes to writing short stories, you might think a writer's success would correspond to how much talent they have, but that's not always true.

It's often how people react to being rejected that makes the difference between success and failure. I've known many talented writers who, if they send out a piece of writing at all, only send it out once. If it gets rejected, or fails to win a prize, they put it away in a drawer.

I write at least fifty stories every year. Many of them get rejected by editors or competition judges. In fact, some get rejected more than once.

I'm not saying that doesn't upset me, of course it does, but over the years I've learned something very important – stories and articles can be rejected for all kinds of reasons. Even great stories can be rejected if they land on an editor's desk at the wrong time.

The aim of this book is to help you come to terms with rejection. It will also increase your chances of an acceptance by highlighting some of the reasons stories don't make the grade.

Once the sales start coming in, you'll find that rejections become much less painful. I've had literally hundreds so I know what I'm talking about!

I write mainly for women's magazines so do bear in mind that much of the advice that follows is geared towards that market.

Now for a bit about me.

I've been writing short stories for a living since 2003 and have sold hundreds to various magazines, both in the UK and overseas.

As well as fiction, I have a column in Writers' Forum each month which is called SHORT STORY SUCCESS where I talk about my life as a writer, offering encouragement and advice.

In November 2011, I finally achieved my ambition to become a novelist when my book, THE MAGIC OF FISHKEEPING was published (available from Amazon ISBN No. 978–3–8454–4538–0).

I live in Leeds in West Yorkshire where I still imagine that, one day, I will find love.

To find out more about me, visit

www.akacatherinehoward.weebly.com or drop by my blog at http://akacatherinehoward.blogspot.com

I am also on Facebook and Twitter as Linda Lewis.

My email address is akacatherinehoward@yahoo.co.uk so if you would like to get in touch, I would love to hear from you.

## REASONS FOR REJECTION.

## NUMBER 1: AIMED AT THE WRONG TARGET

One of the main reasons that editors reject short stories. They are not aimed at the right market.

Market research is essential.

Until you have  read a magazine you have no idea what kind of stories they use.

My main markets at the moment are Take a Break's Fiction Feast, Woman's Weekly, My Weekly, The Weekly News, Yours, Ireland's Own and a few others. Each of these magazines has a different readership.

What I try to do is build up a picture of an 'average' reader in my mind. This involves stereotyping which is not something I normally do, but as a writer, it's an essential skill. I need to know who my readers are and try to give them what they want.

Let me use The People's Friend as an example. If you look at the magazine you will adverts that are clearly aimed at old people, and I don't mean people in their fifties. Adverts are all about being comfortable, comfortable foot wear, comfortable clothes, easy access to baths and so on.

If there are gadgets for sale, they will be the kind of thing that helps to make an older person's life easier, not more complicated so you are unlikely, for example to see an advert for a Blackberry or lap top.

That isn't to say that nobody who reads The People's Friend owns a PC, it merely tells you that keeping up with technology isn't a priority for the majority of readers.

If you look at the stories, they are accompanied by illustrations. These are usually watercolours, nicely done and very tasteful. This gives writers a useful pointer. It tells you that the magazine's readers like to see the things they are reading out so adding more description of people and places will improve your chances of a sale.

Again, looking at the illustrations will provide you with a snapshot of the kind of stories the magazine will include. The pictures are usually soft and sweet, or atmospheric. They are not dark or scary so there's not much point sending them a violent crime thriller.

If I look at Fiction Feast in the same way I will find things are very different.

For a start, the illustrations are in black and white which makes them far more graphic. They are photographs, not painting which again adds to the realism. They are not necessarily nice photos either.

Some of the characters portrayed in them may be ugly, or fat, or repulsive in some way. They may look angry, or upset even violent. This immediately tells you that they are looking for a different type of story. Their readers don't want nostalgia, they want up to date stories with modern themes. This is the place to send your violent crime story to.

Once you've looked at the illustrations and the adverts, it's time to read the stories themselves.

As you do, I find it helps to make a check list. The things I look for when I do this are as follows.

What tense is the story written in – past, or present?

What viewpoint does the writer use – third person, or first person?

Is the main character male or female?

How old is the main character?

What type of story is it?

How much of the story is told in dialogue?

Once you have read all the stories you will end up with an overview.

You should find that if you do this for Fiction Feast most stories will be written in the third person, using the past tense, and told from a woman's point of view, but if you look through a Woman's Weekly Fiction Special, there will be more stories written in the first person and of those, some will be written in the present tense.

It's actually extremely rare to find a first person, present tense story in Take a Break's Fiction Feast, so there's little point sending them one.

This is the kind of information you will gather simply by reading the magazines and studying them.

There's absolutely no point sending a story to a market that it is completely unsuited for. If the market always uses stories that are at least half dialogue they are extremely unlikely to take yours if it is dialogue free.

It is vital to keep on top of market research and analysis as magazines are constantly changing, as they adapt to a changing readership so try not to neglect this very important aspect. It might not be actual writing, but it is vitally important and useful.

## REASONS FOR REJECTION.

## NUMBER 2: THE BEGINNING ISN'T STRONG

It's been said, many times before, that the opening line of a story is very important. It's often called the hook. The first line, paragraph or even page in a longer work, need to grab the reader's attention and make them want to read on.

Many writers make the mistake of starting with a lot of background. They spend time setting the scene or describing the main character. This is fine, in a longer work, but in a short story, you don't have the luxury of space. Also, the shorter a story is, the sooner it needs to get up and running.

For the kind of markets I generally aim for, I find it helps to start in the middle of the action. Ideally, the beginning should also raise unanswered questions.

These are openings from three of my published short stories.

1. *If you want to know what a person is like, take a look at their bookcase. That's what I thought, until I met Melanie Greaves.*

2. *"You do want grandchildren, don't you Rob?"*

3. *Angela frowned at the calendar. At first she convinced herself not to worry. After all, what was one month?*

4. *It's funny how, when you're dreading something, time speeds up.*

The first of these grabs the attention by making an interesting, and sweeping statement.

I don't know about you, but I always have a look at people's books when I go to their house for the first time. I can't help it. Are there lots of books on gardening, or more crime and thrillers? A person's taste in books reveals the things they really enjoy. By simply studying a person's taste in books, we can find out quite a lot about them.

The man in the story goes on to tell us that this rule, that we have taken on board, doesn't apply to one particular woman.

We can't help but be intrigued by this. We want to know who she is, and why she's different from the rest of us.

In the second example, the underlined word is the hook.

We want to know why the word do has been emphasised.

We guess too that the main character is going to be the man, Rob, as he's the one to whom the question has been addressed. As most stories in women's magazines feature a female protagonist, this makes the story more intriguing to a lot of readers.

It also starts with dialogue which has the effect of immediately drawing us into the action.

In the third example, lots of questions are raised. We're led to believe that the woman is worried she might be pregnant, which leads to more questions including, is she married, does she want a baby, how old is she, and so on.

In example four, we can't help wonder what it is the main character is dreading. The other thing that draws us into the story is that we all understand what he means. We've all had that feeling that time can speed up or slow down, according to what is going on. Any shared experience likes that makes a wonderful hook to catch a reader with.

As you can see with example number two, another good way to start a story is by using dialogue.

Dialogue adds immediacy to a story. It is easy to read and adds pace. Not only that, the things people say reveal so much about them. Letting your characters talk to each other can be used instead of large chunks of information. In other words, dialogue helps writers to show, rather than tell.

It's tempting, when you write a story, to start with some of the background, or to spend time setting the scene. If this is something you tend to do, don't worry about it. Get the story written down first and then think about where it should actually start. I often do this myself in the first draft. It helps me to get into the story as most of the time, I don't know for sure how it will all pan out.

The beginning also indicates what kind of a story it is. In other words, is it going to be a romance, or a spooky ghost story. Is it about grown ups or children?

Here's an example, again from one of my published stories.

*Diana started laughing. Telling fortunes at a teenager's party – the idea was preposterous.*

This tells us several things. The story is light hearted. It's about different generations. We also know that, despite her reservations, Diana is going to end up doing precisely that – telling fortunes at a party.

With this knowledge, the reader can immediately decide if this is the kind of story they want to read.

Sometimes, the opening is the last thing I work on. Ideally, I'm looking for a way to tie up the ending and the beginning as that makes the whole thing feel finished, more rounded if you like. Most importantly, though, I want the beginning to raise questions in the reader's mind as that way they will find it hard to resist continuing to read.

If one of your stories has been rejected, take another look at the beginning and ask yourself these questions.

Is it interesting enough?

Does it raise any questions in the reader's mind?

Would starting with dialogue improve it?

Does the start reflect the ending or the title in some way?

In short, make sure that whatever you choose to do, the opening lines of your story are as strong as you can make them.

## REASONS FOR REJECTION.

## NUMBER 3: THE ENDING DOESN'T WORK

I often have no real idea how my story will end when I start writing it. Sometimes I know the beginning and the middle but the only ending I can think of is either dull, or easy to predict. When that happens I normally write the story anyway and see what happens.

It helps to think of a story as having a structure and shape to it.

What you want to produce is a feeling of completeness and one of the best ways to do this is to link the ending with the beginning of the story, either that, or the title.

One of the first stories I sold to Woman's Weekly was called THE WOMAN IN THE BRIGHT RED COAT. It starts with that image in the title, and ends with the same image. This leaves the reader with a satisfied feeling when they reach the final sentence. I also make sure to mention that red coat during the story too. I've underlined these to make them more obvious.

The story follows.

### *THE WOMAN IN THE BRIGHT RED COAT*

*It's just what I need – there's more than two hours left until lunch time, the rain's coming down in buckets, the windscreen wipers are wheezing, and THAT infuriatingly dreadful woman is waiting at the next stop. She's always so cheerful, come rain, snow, sleet or shine.*

*It isn't natural. Not natural at all.*

*For a moment, I think about driving past. I could pretend I haven't seen her, after all, it's only a request stop, but she's waving her umbrella like a flag.*

*Muttering under my breath, I persuade the bus into a lower gear and pull over.*

*"Good morning driver," she says cheerfully as she passes me the correct fare. She always has the correct fare. "Return to the High Street please."*

*I watch her in the mirror as she makes her way down the bus. She seems to know everyone.*

*'Hello Mrs A. How are you Mr B?' It's as though talking has suddenly become infectious, people start chattering away. Before she got on nobody had said a word for ages.*

*"What's she got to be so happy about?" I mutter aloud as I join yet another queue of slow moving traffic.*

*I catch a glimpse of my face in the mirror and scowl.*

*Frowning seems to be the only expression I can find lately. I hardly know what makes me feel so fed up. Anything and everything gets me down - the traffic, the weather, teenagers. And most annoying of all? The smiling woman in the bright red coat.*

*We crawl along to the next stop where a boy offers me a ten pound note for a fifty pence fare. He can't be more than fourteen but he's already as tall as me. He reminds me of a mop with his floppy blond hair.*

*"I can't change that. Can't you read? " I say pointing at the sign which says 'Please have the correct fare ready' in four inch high letters. "Haven't you got anything smaller?"*

*The boy searches his pockets. "No. Sorry."*

*I sense a brief moment of triumph. "You'll have to walk then, won't you?"*

*"But it's nearly a mile to school," he protests. "It's chucking it down. I'll get soaked."*

*But I don't care, I'm fed up, why shouldn't he be miserable too? In fact, why shouldn't everyone be miserable. "Getting wet won't hurt you. It's only water," I tell him.*

*He's about to get off when a voice comes from behind my left ear. "Here's fifty p. Let me pay your fare." It's Mrs red raincoat herself.*

*"Thanks, Mrs Parsons. I'll pay you back," says the youth grinning happily. He makes faces at me as he swaggers down the bus.*

*"You won't see that money again," I tell her, but she just laughs.*

*"So what?" she says. "It's only 50p."*

*I glare at her retreating figure in the mirror. Nothing gets her down. It's too much, and why can't she wear sensible clothes, I mean who wears a bright red raincoat at her age. She must be in her fifties, for goodness sake.*

*When I see her again two days later, the sun is shining weakly so there's no red coat, instead she's wearing blue. It's not just any blue, it's an 'in your face' peacock blue. I can hardly believe anybody would make a coat that colour, let alone want to wear one. I can't resist asking if the boy has paid her back her fifty pence.*

*" Not yet," she says, giving me a broad smile, "But I'm sure he will do."*

*"Thought not," I reply, trying not to sound too gleeful.*

*She stares hard at me, as though it was me who'd done something wrong, not the teenager. "Why are you always so bad tempered?" she says.*

*"I'm not."*

*"You are. You sit there, muttering under your breath like somebody from that television programme, what's it called?" She thinks for a moment. "Ah yes, I remember - Grumpy Old Men.."*

*I don't bother to reply. After all, what is there to smile about? The council tax is going up, again. There's never anything worth watching on TV. I'm nearly sixty. I hate my job. Hate living on my own. It's all right for her. She's happy and I'm not. That's all there is to it.*

*It's more than a week before I see her again. I think about asking where she's been but I don't.*

*"The boy paid me back that fare," she tells me as she takes her ticket.*

*"Oh." I can't think of anything else to say.*

*I wait for her to take her usual place at the back of the bus, but she doesn't. She sits on the seat closest to me.*

*"I've been thinking about you," she says, "wondering why you're always so fed up. I've decided to try and cheer you up."*

*"Don't bother," I snap back. "I'm fine the way I am."*

*I expect that to shut her up but it doesn't, instead she chatters away to me for the whole journey. She talks about her grandchildren, her cat, and somebody called Jack. I guess he must be her husband.*

*I try not to, but her enthusiasm is hard to resist. I catch myself smiling.*

*"You should do that more often," she says. "It suits you."*

*I don't mean to, but the words are out before I can stop them. Rude, hateful words. Her smile fades and I can see that I've hurt her, only that doesn't make me feel good, it makes me feel worse. Much worse.*

*That evening I find myself standing in front of the mirror, trying out a smile. It feels strange. Unnatural. I pull my lips back into a more familiar snarl. So what if I am a grumpy old man? Why shouldn't I be if I want to?*

*There's no sign of her for the next few days. When I do finally see her, it's a Sunday and the bus is almost empty. I have to stop myself from grinning. It's only then that I realise how much I've been missing her.*

*She sits down, close to me, but she doesn't say a word. As the minutes pass I feel more and more uncomfortable. If she doesn't say something soon it will be time for her to get off.*

*"Lost your tongue," I say at last.*

*"Sorry," she says. "I thought you were too grumpy to speak to anyone."*

*"I'm not grumpy, it's just that everything gets me down lately. Getting older, aches and pains, the weather, my job."*

*She sighs. "You should try living a bit more. Do some voluntary work like me, then you'll be too busy to worry about a few stiff joints."*

*I try to think of something clever to say but I can't. "At least you don't live on your own," I reply sulkily.*

*"No, I don't. I wouldn't want to."*

*I relax a little. That's a definite point to me. "My wife died four years ago," I tell her. "It's all right for you, you've got your husband to keep you company."*

*Her smile fades for a moment. "I'm a widow. My husband passed away in 1999."*

*I don't know what to say, that wasn't what I'm expecting. "I'm so sorry, but I thought….." I struggle to find the words. "But then who's Jack? I've heard you talking about him. Is he your son?"*

*She laughs and the light comes back to her grey eyes. "Good heavens no. My son lives in Kent. Jack just lives with me. Oops!" she says as she laughs again. "I mean he just rents a room, he's a student. Hearing his music helps keep me young."*

*"I can't stand modern music," I complain to her. "It's just noise."*

*"Have you ever listened to it?" she asks me as she gets off the bus.*

*I don't answer, I'm much too busy thinking. I'm still thinking when I get home. I tour the house, imagining the rooms as they once were, filled with laughter. What a waste of space, I hear myself saying, and I don't mean just the house.*

*That evening I go through all my usual reasons for being miserable, but each time I hear Mrs P's voice in my head countering them. I know she's right. It's up to me. I can rattle around in an empty house, feeling bored, or I can do something about it.*

*With a pang I realise it's been almost two years since my daughter and her family came to stay, longer since my son came home. The next morning it's raining again. Mrs P pulls out a bag from the pocket of her red raincoat and hands it to me as she gets on the bus.*

*"Listen to this CD," she says, "then tell me you don't like today's music."*

*I put it on while I eat my dinner. I'm determined not to enjoy it one little bit, only some of the tracks are rather catchy. One of them sticks so hard in my head I find myself singing it as I wash up.*

*I look at the cover. Norah Jones, R.E.M, Robbie Williams, the list goes on. I've never even heard of some of them.*

*"Thanks, Mrs P," I say, when I gave her the disc back a couple of days later. "I really enjoyed it. Especially that R.E.M track."*

*"Great," she says "I'll lend you another one." Then she looks at me, smiles and says "And it's about time you stopped calling me Mrs P. My name's Sara."*

*That evening the telephone rings. It's my daughter, Carly, doing her duty, making her once a month call.*

*"How are you Dad?" she asks me. I can almost hear her taking a deep breath, preparing herself for my usual lengthy list of complaints.*

*I open my mouth, ready to tell her about my bad toe, the traffic jams, and the never ending rain, but as I do, the image of a bright red raincoat pops into my head.*

*"I'm fine lass," I say with a smile. "You see, I've met a wonderful woman."*

This story also demonstrates another very important point about endings, and that's knowing WHEN to stop. I could have carried on with the story, having the couple go on a date, or even get married, but there was no need.

I've made it clear that a romance is on the cards, and that was all I needed to do. It's often better to let the reader decide what happens next. That way they feel more involved with the story and are more likely to enjoy it, and remember it.

Many years ago, somebody told me this – start a story late, and finish it early, and that really was excellent advice. It also applies to things like radio plays where you need to make sure the listener doesn't switch channels.

## REASONS FOR REJECTION.

## NUMBER 4 : POOR DIALOGUE

Writing good dialogue may look simple but it's actually one of the hardest things to do.

If your characters conversations don't sound realistic or are stilted and old fashioned, this may be enough to cause it to be rejected.

The best way to test whether dialogue is working is to read it out loud. If it's difficult to read, then it probably needs work. Generally speaking, less is more. In other words, try to beak up dialogue into small chunks rather than long speeches. Speeches belong in plays, not short stories.

If you struggle with dialogue, try to listen to other people speaking whenever and wherever you can. You will find that, for the most part, people speak in half sentences and phrases.

As well as the words they use, notice what they are doing while they speak. It's rare to find somebody who is just talking. There is usually some kind of action, even if it's just a change of expression, to accompany dialogue. Also, people interrupt each other all the time.

Look at your dialogue. If it appears as large blocks on the page, each several lines long, this could be why the story was rejected.

The following story is all dialogue. It's a conversation that takes place between a mother and daughter over the phone.

See how short the various exchanges are and how I've used actions and thoughts to break up the dialogue to keep it from becoming too static.

*Sandy took a deep breath then picked up the phone. This wasn't going to be easy. "Hi Mum. It's me."*

*"Oh hello dear. How are you?"*

*"I'm fine. Look. I've got something to tell you. Are you sitting down?"*

*"No. Should I be?"*

*"Probably, " said Sandy.*

*"There's nothing wrong is there? You're not ill are you?" she asked, a note of anxiety in her voice.*

*"No I'm fine." Sandy laughed nervously. "Are you sitting down yet Mum?"*

*"OK I've sat down on the stairs. Go on. Tell me what's happened."*

*"Well, it's not bad news, it's good news."*

*"Go on then, hit me." There were times when her mother's choice of words made Sandy smile.*

*Sandy took another deep breath before going on. "You know Mitch Carter? The man who runs the garage."*

*"Yes. Of course. Everyone knows Mitch. It would be hard not to."*

*"Well," she paused again before blurting out her news. She already had a pretty good idea what her mother's reaction was going to be. "We're getting married in May."*

*"Goodness gracious me! What about poor Daniel? You've been going out with him ever since you broke up with Steve. I thought you two were happy."*

*"Well, we were, for a while. He's got a good job, he's honest, and he loves me to bits, but, frankly, he's a bit boring. I want some excitement in my life. You remember the Christmas party, down the pub?"*

*"Yes. It was a bit noisy as far as I can remember. "*

*"Well it all started there. As you know, Daniel couldn't go, he was on call with the Gas Board. I got chatting with Mitch and before I knew it, we were kissing. We've been having a secret affair ever since."*

*"Ah, that explains a few things. I wondered what was going on. You kept working all those late nights, and making sudden extra shopping trips, I thought your memory was going, like mine."*

*"There's nothing wrong with your memory Mum. I bet you could name every man I've dated since I left home."*

*"True, I could to. I must admit, you certainly have an interesting love life. Anyway, tell me all about it. I was under the impression you were happy with Daniel. I didn't think you liked Mitch, let alone wanted to marry him."*

*"I don't exactly LIKE him, I just can' resist him. He's got this animal magnetism. All he has to do is look at a girl and they melt inside. It's really strange. When he looks at me that way, I'd do anything for him."*

*"Huh! Well it all seems a bit sudden to me. You've only just got your divorce through from Steve. I felt so sorry for him when you left."*

*"Everyone did. I was definitely the guilty party there, no mistake, but that's life. It's just the way it is these days. Out of one relationship straight into the next. You must admit, he got over it pretty quickly. Julie's expecting a baby, any day now."*

*"I know dear, " she sighed, "but it all seems wrong somehow. Your dad and me were married forty years." Her mother's voice grew more wistful "It wasn't all plain sailing you know."*

*"I know Mum, you told me Mum. Besides, I was there."*

*"But we stuck it out. Once your father realised how unhappy I was, he agreed to go to Marriage Guidance with me. We came through our problems, stronger than ever."*

*"You were lucky Mum."*

*"Luck had nothing to do with it. I worked hard to keep that marriage together, and so did your father. If only young people these days took time to*

*talk to each other. One bad patch and they're off. I mean, you and Steve were only married ten months. Why didn't you go to Relate, or whatever it is they call themselves these days?"*

*"There was no point. It was a mistake from day one. We should never have got married."*

*"You can say that again. I told you he wasn't the right man for you."*

*"I know you did mum, but I felt I had to marry him. I was pregnant."*

*"Yes but when you had that accident and lost the baby, six weeks before the wedding. That was so terribly sad. I expected you to call it off." She sighed wearily. "This thing with Mitch. Can't you change your mind? Stick with Daniel. OK, so Mitch is attractive and sexy, I know that, but there's something about him I don't like. He's been married three times already, hasn't he?"*

*"Four."*

*"Four! And how old is he. 41, 42?"*

*"About that."*

*"Well! Of course I know nothing I say will make any difference. It never does. You'll get married anyway."*

*"Sorry Mum, but the ceremony's already booked. We're holding the reception in the pub."*

*"Again! I'd have thought you'd seen enough of the place. Anyway, thanks for letting me know. You're a good girl really, despite what they say." Her mother's voice lowered to a whisper. "Tell me dear, will this marriage last, or don't you know yet?"*

*"If I tell you, you have to promise not to breathe a word. It's a huge secret."*

*"OK. I promise."*

*"As we leave the reception, Mitch spots an old friend, Samuel Beasley, who he hasn't seen for years. He dashes across the road without looking and gets knocked down and badly injured. I spend the next episode by his bedside, being comforted by Samuel."*

*"Don't tell me. Let me guess. Mitch dies and you marry his best friend."*

*"You've got it, Mum. That's life in Soapland for you. "*

*"Well thanks for letting me know. And if the writers want a believable story line, you can always get them to come and talk to me."*

*"Don't worry Mum, I'll do that. Goodbye."*

As you can see, both characters do make the odd lengthy speech but most of the time, the dialogue is short and snappy. Variations like this help to make dialogue 'sound' real.

The fact is it's not real at all. If we wrote down people's conversations as they happen we would soon discover that people hesitate, pause and repeat themselves all the time. If we copied that word for word, our stories would suffer.

It's not 'reality' were aiming for rather something that gives the impression of reality.

Above all, it has to be easy to read so if your dialogue is full of long sentences, try breaking them up into shorter ones. That could make all the difference.

## REASONS FOR REJECTION.
## NUMBER 5: TOO PREDICTABLE

Does your story have any surprises or is it all too easy to work out what happens right from the outset?

Maybe you have a story where boy meets girl and they get off on the wrong foot. Readers will assume that, in the end, romance will blossom. Unless you find a fresh and original way to tell the story, it may not be a satisfying read. Editors and judges are looking for something different, some new way of telling an old story.

What you need to do is make the journey interesting. In other words, add some twists and turns, or put some obstacles in the character's way before reaching a satisfying conclusion. Another way is to use an unusual setting, or set the story in the past or even the future.

Think of Shakespeare for a moment. The Forbidden Planet is simply a sci fi version of The Tempest. Westside Story is Romeo and Juliet moved to twentieth century America.

In each case we have a good idea what is going to happen, but because the setting is different, that over comes any predictability.

## REASONS FOR REJECTION.

## NUMBER 6: TOO MUCH TELLING.

Show, don't tell.

This is something else that writers are told to do all the time.

Many people struggle with this as it's not an easy distinction to make. When we tell a story, that normally means that we let the reader know what's going on by describing events as though from a distance. An example might be as follows.

*Ted wondered what the note his wife had left, propped up on the kitchen table, actually meant.*

Here I have simply told you how he's feeling and what has happened. If I show you, the effect is very different.

*Ted picked up the piece of paper. As he read the note, the colour drained from his face. Surely Jane didn't mean it, did she?*

The second example is more like a scene, in other words, Ted is doing something. We can picture Ted, picking up that note and reading it. That makes the writing more immediate. We're not just being told about it after the event, we're in the here and now.

Dialogue is another great way of showing. When characters say something, we can hear in our minds what is going on.

Have a look at one of your rejected stories. If it is too 'telly' it will probably lack pace and feel slow to read. If that's the case why not see if it can be improved by injecting some dialogue.

As you write, ask yourself, can the reader hear or picture this in their minds? If the answer is no, you are probably doing too much telling.

## REASONS FOR REJECTION.
## NUMBER 7: A SURPRISE RATHER THAN A TWIST

“It was all a dream.”

As you read an intriguing story, you find yourself desperately wanting to see what happens at the end. You’ve racked your brains and can’t think how the protagonist will solve their problem or escape their predicament, and then you’re told it was all a dream. Imagine how disappointed you would feel, cheated even.

Surprise endings are very popular with magazine fiction editors, and with their readers, but the surprise has to be believable. In other words, when they look back through the story, the reader needs to be able to spot the clues, that hopefully, due to your skill as a writer, they have missed.

It’s a bit like writing a murder mystery. If the murderer turned out to be somebody who didn’t even appear in the book, or was only introduced three pages from the end, crime fans would be very upset. They read crime fiction because they want to have a chance of working out the ending for themselves. Any ‘surprise’ must have been foreshadowed. You can’t just pull an ending out of the hat.

If your rejected story has a twist, look at it carefully and ask yourself these questions.

Is it possible, from the clues, to work out the twist?

Are the clues sufficiently well hidden to make guessing the twist difficult enough?

If the answer to both questions is yes, that’s great, but you still need to ask yourself one more thing - is it too easy to guess the twist?

As you can see, the hard part is getting the balance right. It must be difficult to spot the surprise ending before it comes but not impossible.

See if you can spot the twist coming in this story. It was first published in Woman's Weekly.

*A BIT OF PAMPERING*

*"Hang on a minute," said Matt. "You've already ticked half a dozen boxes. We'll be running round like headless chickens."*

*"I know, but this isn't something we do every day." Sharon took Matt's hand in hers. "We deserve a bit of pampering."*

*She didn't need to say anything else. They'd been through hell during the past year – every day, a waking nightmare.*

*It started when she found the lump.*

*Her first instinct was to ignore it and hope it would go away. It was lucky she didn't because the lump was cancerous. If it had been left much longer, the outcome could have been fatal. It was grim enough as it was.*

*The cancer had been caught early, but it proved a stubborn foe. For the last ten months, she'd felt as though her life wasn't her own. Every week, every day, every hour had to be planned around the disease.*

*Tests, injections, chemotherapy, good days, bad days, days when she was so completely tried and exhausted she began to wonder if she had the strength to carry on. Now, at last, the fight was over, and she and Matt could pick up their lives again. It was his idea to book a holiday. A bit of pampering was just what she needed.*

*The hotel offered a wide range of activities and spa treatments. They were working their way through the leaflet, deciding what to choose. While she had the various massages and other treatments, Matt could spend his time swimming, or using the gym. They'd even signed up for a course of archery lessons, held in the hotel's extensive grounds.*

*As she ticked another box, she read out the description to Matt. "Why not try our mud wrap? Designed to cleanse, detoxify and revitalise the skin." She giggled. "Sounds like fun, don't you think?"*

*Matt nodded and pointed at the form. "What's that one all about? Colour me beautiful?"*

*Sharon snuggled up to him. "You know Gloria Stevens? The woman who works in the children's library?"*

*He nodded. "She always wore black and suddenly she's wearing nothing but pinks and purples."*

*She sat up straight. "See, you do notice what people wear," she teased.*

*"It's hard not to in her case," admitted Matt. "She used to look like Anne Robinson on the Weakest Link. Nothing but black. I thought she was in mourning."*

*"Well, she had one of these consultations. The woman told her that black didn't suit her. From that day, she stopped wearing it. She took all her old clothes to the charity shop."*

*Matt pretended to frown. "I see. This is just an excuse to buy a whole new wardrobe when we get home."*

*Sharon laughed. "I've lost so much weight over the past few months, I'm going to need one anyway. Unless you want me to walk about naked."*

*He gave her a wicked leer. "Suits me," he said.*

*"Behave yourself," she said as she turned the form over. "Do you think I should have a makeover?"*

*"You don't need one. You're perfect just the way you are."*

*"Right answer, but all the same." She ran a hand through her hair. "Maybe I could have my hair done."*

*"Whatever you want," he said. "This break is for you, remember?"*

*"The seaweed massage sounds interesting."*

*Matt wrinkled his nose in disgust. "Don't come near me if you have one of those. I can't stand seaweed. It stinks."*

*Sharon elbowed him playfully in the ribs. "I'm sure it doesn't smell bad, silly, or nobody would have it done." She was about to tick the box when he stopped her.*

*"Why don't you leave it there? You can always sign up for more things once we're there," he said. "This is meant to be a treat. I don't want you wearing yourself out."*

*She hugged him. "Sorry, you're right. I guess I got carried away. There," she put down the pen, and popped the booking form in the envelope. "I can't wait, can you?"*

*"You deserve it, he said. "I don't know what I'd do without you."*

*A week later, Sharon started to have second thoughts. The idea of a pampering holiday had sounded perfect, but now she realised that it was a different type of holiday she wanted.*

*She had a word with Matt. "About the holiday," she said.*

*Luckily they were able to change their booking with no problems. Soon, Sharon found herself in Majorca, stretched out by the pool, soaking up the warm September sunshine, happy to watch other people playing ball and swimming up and down.*

*She shut her eyes, and began to doze, not even bothering to read, until a drop of water fell onto her nose, waking her.*

*"Fancy a bite to eat?" Matt stood over her, his hair still wet from the pool.*

*She nodded.*

*"Good. Let's go to our room. I need to shower and get changed." He pulled her to her feet. "You've been lying there for hours."*

*She took his hand. "I know. Isn't it fabulous?"*

*He laughed and put his arm round her waist. "Hey! You're soaking wet," she complained, but she was smiling.*

*Matt looked a picture of health. It was hard to believe that he'd been so poorly. She'd worked night and day, nursing and taking care of him, keeping his spirits up so that he could beat the illness. It was only when the doctors gave him the all clear that she realised how hard it had been on her as well as him. She'd lost so much weight and felt completely exhausted.*

*Spa treatments and massages were all very well, but for the next seven days, she knew exactly what she wanted to do - absolutely nothing.*

Hopefully I will have fooled you into thinking two things. Firstly that it was the woman who had the lump, and secondly that she wants the holiday to help her recover after all she's been through whereas what has actually happened is that it was her husband who was ill. She needs the holiday for a well earned rest having looked after him so well. .

If I did manage to fool you, I did it by using your assumptions to trip you up and lead you down the wrong path.

The story is in women's magazine. The main, viewpoint character is female. A lump is found. It's no wonder you think she has breast cancer but if you look back through the story you will find that I never say who had the lump or even where it was. I let the reader fill in the (wrong) information for themselves.

## REASONS FOR REJECTION.

## NUMBER 8: BAD TIMING

Lead times for magazines vary enormously. Even weeklies start work on seasonal specials several months in advance. If you send a Christmas story off in November, you will probably be too late.

The simple fact is this. If an editor needs five Christmassy stories and they've already bought five, yours is very unlikely to be considered, let alone purchased.

You need to send in stories well ahead of time. That means starting to write about snow and Christmas trees when it's still warm and sunny outside and to start thinking of holiday stories in February.

Sending stories out too early is much better than too late.

If one of your seasonal stories has been rejected, and you can't see any other reason why that happened, you may just have been unlucky with your timing. If that's the case, send it out again next year, only a month or two earlier.

## REASONS FOR REJECTION.

## NUMBER 9: LACK OF, OR WELL USED, THEME

Sometimes stories are rejected because they don't have an obvious theme.

What this means is simple - what is the story REALLY about? Is it about lost love, jealousy, or revenge? Is there a message? For example, this might be a proverb such as Absence makes the heart grow fonder, or Two Wrongs don't make a right.

Have a look at a rejected story and ask yourself what it was you were trying to say. Do you know? If you do know, did you succeed in getting your message across?

Having a clear theme in your head as you write helps to makes sure that a story stays on track and that it has a shape to it.

There are certain themes that crop up over and over again. Sometimes this is the result of current events. For example, when the Twilight series of books and films came out, editors received an enormous number of stories about vampires. This can make them very jaded so that even a superb story about vampires will be rejected.

Other themes have gone out of fashion. One of these is the twist ending where the main character turns out to be some kind of animal or plant. These used to be very popular but are now very hard to place.

The following quote comes from a letter sent to regular contributors to Woman's Weekly.

'No more "retired/redundant hubby getting under my feet"; adopted children being reunited with their mothers and brides with cold feet until further notice, please.'

In 2010 they said this.

'We're receiving a lot of stories about women "finding themselves" in midlife by doing bungee jumps, hot air balloon rides and so on. There's also a bit too much about death, illness and people sorting out their parents' houses after they've died.'

Unfortunately it's hard for writers to know what the trends are as some are not easy to spot.

The good news is this. However well used a theme might be, if you can tell the story in a fresh and original way, it might still gain you a sale.

## REASONS FOR REJECTION.

## NUMBER 10: REAL LIFE VS FICTION

It can hurt when a story is rejected and it's been based on events that actually happened to you.

Sadly, just because something is true, that doesn't mean it will make a good short story.

Life is full of coincidences. How many of us have been on holiday only to come across somebody we knew at school, or who lives less than a mile away? This kind of thing happens all the time, but it does NOT make a good story.

The most satisfying stories are those that have a structure to them. By this I mean that events are linked. One thing happens, and that causes the next thing to happen. In real life, this isn't necessarily the case. People can go off on a tangent, be distracted, win the lottery and so on.

In a work of fiction, things need to be more focussed so take that true story of yours and change something important about it. With luck, that should be enough to allow your imagination room to work, and prevent you from reproducing reality too closely

## REASONS FOR REJECTION.

## NUMBER 11: IS IT A STORY OR AN ANECDOTE?

Does your story have a structure, or is it merely a series of events as in an anecdote?

This is a problem that many writers struggle with. It's the reason why jokes seldom translate into good stories.

Writers are often told that stories need conflict. In this case, conflict simply means that there is some kind of problem or difficulty that the characters face and which they try to solve, not always successfully, as the story progresses. The problem can be big, like coping with loss, or tiny, like losing a watch. It can simply be a decision that needs to be made.

The trick is to make things difficult for your characters. If they have a problem and solve it easily, that can make for a dull and uninteresting read so try to make things more difficult for them.

Let me give you an example.

Mary is on a cruise. She discovers that the man dining at the next table is her first love who she lost touch with when his family moved away. They fall in love again, and get married.

That won't make a good story. It's all too easy. We need to put some more obstacles in the way.

Mary is on a cruise with a male friend She discovers that the man dining at the next table is her first love who she lost touch with when his family moved away. The problem is, he isn't alone. Mary asks her friend to pretend to be her husband or boyfriend, only to find you that her lost love is actually unmarried and is on a singles holiday.

Now Mary has a problem to solve and you have the makings of a story.

Here's another example.

Susan puts an ad in the Lonely Hearts column in the local paper. She meets Brian, falls in love and gets married.

That's all very nice for Susan, but it's not exactly interesting is it?

What you want is something like this.

Susan puts an ad in the Lonely Hearts column in the local paper. She meets two men, both of whom she likes very much. They both like her too. What happens next?

## REASONS FOR REJECTION.

## NUMBER 12: TWO DIMENSIONAL CHARACTERS

Many people will say, myself included, that for them the most important part of any story, be it a thousand worder or a novel, is the main character or characters.

If a reader believes in a character, they will care what happens to them and keep reading. To achieve this make sure your characters are neither too good or too evil. Either can become boring.

Often what makes characters interesting are their faults so make sure your hero isn't too perfect. After all, there really is no such thing as a perfect man, or woman for that matter.

If you struggle with this, why not give the character a hobby or interest that you wouldn't expect a person of that gender to indulge in? For example, a policeman who likes to knit, or a woman who has a model train set. This one change will immediately give them greater depth and make them a lot more interesting.

## REASONS FOR REJECTION.

## NUMBER 13: TOO MANY CHARACTERS

If you have too many characters in your story, that may make it feel muddled and confusing to read. The number of named characters a story can comfortably support is governed, largely, by the word count.

Sadly there isn't a mathematical formula and if there was, I probably would not use it. What you need to do instead is use your common sense. As a general rule, have as few characters as you can get away with.

Earlier I made the distinction of saying named characters. The reason I did this is that more often than not, it's the extra names that become confusing.

Names stand out. They make a reader stop and think, who is the person? If they keep having to do that, even though it's happening on an unconscious level, their enjoyment will be adversely affected.

Make a list of all the named characters and ask yourself this question – do I need to give them a name? You might find that Joe can be referred to as the shop keeper, and Meg can be called the teacher. Each name you lose will make the story easy to follow and reduce any confusion.

If you find you have too many characters, this may be a symptom for another problem. It might mean that you have gone off on a tangent, moving away from the people you started the story with. As a general rule, whoever you started the story with, end with them too.

## REASONS FOR REJECTION.
## NUMBER 14: CONFUSING NAMES

If characters' names begin with the same letter, for example, Joseph and Joanne, Mike and Mark, or sound similar like Wendy and Cindy, readers can become confused as to who is who.

This is an easy trap to fall into. Fortunately, it's also an easy one to fix.

Unless there's an important reason why names need to be similar, it's better to make characters' names as different from each other as you can.

If you are writing about people you know, or are basing characters on family members who have similar sounding names, you can get round this problem very easily. Simply write your story using the actual names, then when you get to the end, use Control F to find the names and replace them with different ones. It takes just moments to do.

Do be careful though.

If you have chosen a name like Ann, words such as t**ann**ing will be highlighted too. In that case you will need to replace them one a time, not all at once.

## REASONS FOR REJECTION.
## NUMBER 15: THE WORD COUNT

It's vital to know how many words your story contains.

Editors have pages to fill and each page needs a certain number of words to fill it. If your story is the wrong length, for example if it runs at one and a half pages and they only have a two page slot to fill, then it will be rejected.

This is also very important when it comes to competitions.

If the word count stated on the entry form is 2000 words, and your story is 2100 words long, the organizers will be within their rights to disqualify it. They MAY not. They may allow a margin of plus or minus five or ten per cent, but why take the risk? It's almost always possible to cut words out of a story, all it takes is practise.

If you use a computer, your word processing programme will probably include a word count facility. These are accurate enough to do the job for you.

If you don't have this facility, you can easily work out an approximate word count by following this simple calculation. Take an average of the number of words in a line by counting the words in ten lines and dividing the total by ten. Next count the number of lines on a page. Now multiply the resulting numbers together and that will give you an average number of words on each page. Then all you have to do is multiply this by the number of pages.

Remember though that this will not be completely accurate so take care to come in slightly under the required word count when entering a competition.

With magazines, plus or minus five percent does not present a problem as most fiction editors will be happy to adjust the length to suit if required.

## REASONS FOR REJECTION.

## NUMBER 16: WHOSE STORY IS IT?

Stories are often rejected because it's unclear who the main character is.

It may start out as being the husband's story, but half way down the page, we're suddenly inside the wife's head, sharing her thoughts.

When the viewpoint keeps switching between lots of different characters, or even just one or two, it can be very confusing for the reader. This problem is exacerbated when a story is very short.

As with any 'rule' there are exceptions.

A talented writer can switch between various viewpoints with relative ease, and still leave the reader in no doubt what's going on, but that is a skill. If you aren't very experienced, all you will do when you switch viewpoints is make life more difficult for yourself.

You need to make up your mind WHO the story is really about and start and end with that person. If at all possible, stay with their viewpoint throughout the whole story. In other words, tell the story as they see it. Don't give other characters' thoughts and opinions except in dialogue.

If the story needs to be told, or is best told, from two different viewpoints, you can make this work by dividing the story into chunks, making it clear when the changes occur.

I use a short line of stars to indicate this as in the following example, taken from my story GROWING PAINS which was published by Woman's Weekly.

*I didn't mean to upset her, all I said was "You're doing that all wrong. You need to leave the tops showing."*

*I hate to see a woman cry. My late wife used to take advantage of that, could turn on the tears like a tap. It was just one of the six million things I loved about her. If this was Mary I'd just give her a big hug and everything would be fine, only this isn't my wife. This woman is a stranger and I have no idea what to do or say, so I just walk away.*

*I tell myself it doesn't matter. The woman is obviously a beginner. All I did was point out a simple mistake. What was I supposed to do, say nothing, then tell her later why she didn't get a crop?*

*It's not long before my work is finished. I pick a plump Savoy cabbage and the last of the Swedes, and head back towards the gate.*

*The new woman was still there. At least she's stopped crying; only I can't help noticing that she is still burying her onion sets way too deep.*

* * * * *

*I blink away the tears and carry on planting my onions until the man leaves. I feel such a fool, for crying, but I can't help myself. It wasn't my idea to have an allotment. I've never been one for making things grow.*

*I'd meant to take extra care, read the label, follow the instructions to the letter, but it blew away in a sudden gust of wind. Maybe the man is wrong. After all, you bury daffodils and they look a lot like onions.*

*As soon as I get indoors, I head straight for the nearest gardening book.*

*My heart sinks as I read the words 'take care to leave the tips of onion sets showing or they will simply rot away. '*

The story switches back and forth between the man and the woman all the way through. In my opinion, this story wouldn't work half as well without this device as it enables the reader to see what the other person makes of the situation.

Sometimes, when I have an idea for a story, I'm not sure who the main character is going to be. I might start writing from a woman's point of view, but by the end of the first draft, I might decide to change it to the man's, or, as in the previous example, use two characters to tell the story.

If you feel that a story isn't working why not see if you can tell it another way by having a different person as the main character. For example, I recently wrote a story based on Cinderella where one of the ugly sisters is the narrator.

Also, have another look at the viewpoint. Some stories work better in the first person, others in the third.

You may find that making a change as simple as that may be all you need to do to turn a rejection into an acceptance.

## REASONS FOR REJECTION.
## NUMBER 17: PRESENTATION

Even if you have never had anything published in your life, it helps if you present your work like a professional.

This means a clean, manuscript with no mistakes or corrections.

Again, unless you are entering a competition when following the guidelines to the letter is vital, there aren't really any rules, it's down to common sense. Use A4, white paper, with at least a 2cm margin all the way round, and choose a straightforward rather than a fancy font. Courier, Ariel, Times New Roman and this one, Garmond, are all good choices. As regards font size, yes, it is important. Aim for 11 as a minimum, 12 if you have plenty of paper to spare.

To save paper, I often use one and a half line spacing but it's better to stick with double spacing if you can.

What you're aiming for is a manuscript that is clear and easy to read.

If you've spilled coffee on the top page, or if there are numerous crossings outs, print off another copy. Selling stories is often about that all important first impression and if your story doesn't look good, that may affect the way the editor or judge perceives it as they read. The don't know that you are an amateur with no published stories under your belt so present your work as though you are a professional and achieve that vital good first impression.

Clever tricks, designed to make your manuscript stand out, like using pink or yellow paper, overly large fonts or using capital letters are a definite no no.

## REASONS FOR REJECTION.

## NUMBER 18: POOR PROOF READING

This is one job I hate.

I find it really hard to spot mistakes in my own work. Spell checkers can only go so far so DON'T rely on them completely.

There are only two ways to make sure you spot every mistake and they are to get somebody else to proof read for you, or read your work out loud.

I use a piece of free software called READPLEASE 2003. It's very easy to use and can be found by a simple internet search.

All you do is cut and paste your words into the space provided, select a male or female voice and the speed you want the story read, and the programme will read your story to you.

I sit there, listening to the voice, with a copy of the story on my desk, noting down any changes I need to make. READPLEASE not only helps me spot spelling mistakes it also helps me to spot repeated words and phrases.

I'd be lost without it.

A manuscript that is peppered with mistakes is not only hard to read it makes it look as though you don't care enough about your writing. This is not the impression you want to make. .

## REASONS FOR REJECTION.
## NUMBER 19: THE STORY IS NOT GOOD ENOUGH

So far we've looked at a whole list of things that may be causing your work to be rejected, but there may be a deeper, underlying reason – it may be the fault of your writing.

The problem here is that unless you get some feedback, you could carry on making the same mistakes, over and over again. Letting your friends and family read and comment on your work is all well and good but unless they are prepared to be brutally honest, the only criticism they give you is likely to be positive.

For feedback to be valuable it needs to come from somebody who knows about the market you are aiming for, and who will give you good, constructive advice, whilst at the same time pointing out any problems with your writing. They should also offer advice to help you improve.

When I lived in Exeter, I joined the writers' circle. Amongst the members were two women who were selling stories to women's magazines, one on a very regular basis, the other occasionally. I asked them both to give me some feedback.

This was enormously valuable. Stories I thought were fine proved to have major errors in them, errors that I was completely unaware of. I learned so much from those two ladies. So if you belong to a group and somebody there is doing better than you are, have a word with them, and see if they are willing to help you. Overall, writers are a generous bunch so don't be afraid to ask. The worst that can happen is they say no.

Beware of feedback from people who don't understand the market you are aiming for. In the same way that not all books are the same, neither are short stories. Make sure the person knows what they are talking about.

When you get feedback, try not to be defensive. Listen first. Ask questions later. If what you are told is painful, that's a good sign, it means you are learning.

I offer an affordable feedback service for short story writers, details of which can be found on my web site but before resorting to paying for somebody's help, why not see if you can find it for free?

Joining writers' groups is not only good for your writing, it's also a great way to find friends and discover new markets, plus it's better than staying home and watching TV.

If there isn't a group in your area, try the internet, or think about setting up your own group. If you are over fifty, your local U3A is a good place to start.

## FINALLY, IT MAY NOT BE YOUR FAULT.

You may have written a perfectly good story that ticks all the right boxes but it might still be rejected.

Some of the reasons for this annoying phenomenon follow. It may simply be bad luck with your timing. The editor may have just bought a story with a similar theme and feel that they can't use another one at that time.

If your story is seasonal, for example if it's a Valentine's Day story, the editor may need a set number of stories with February 14th as the theme. If they need four and have purchased four already, the fifth one to turn up is going to be unlucky. If it's REALLY good, they may hold on to it for the following year but the more likely result will be a rejection.

Sometimes there really is nothing wrong with your story, you've just been unlucky. For example, if the editor or judge has a boss they can't stand, and he has the same name as your hero, this may cloud their judgement. Somebody even told me once they didn't like my story because the hero had a beard and they didn't like beards.

Then there are competitions. If there is a set theme, this will narrow down the range of stories that a judge has to read. For example, if the theme is lost love, there may be several entries with broadly similar plots. If your story is read after a similar one, its impact will be lessened. That's why, when there's a theme, I suggest rejecting the first idea that comes to mind because it will probably have occurred to lots of other people too.

## HOW TO DEAL WITH THE PAIN

Rejections are part of writing. Even brilliant writers have had their stories and books rejected but they didn't let that stop them. They persevered. If they hadn't, nobody would have heard of Harry Potter or Watership Down.

As I said at the beginning, I have had a lot of rejections over the years. The way I deal with them is simple. When a story comes back I try my best to send it somewhere else inside forty eight hours. That way it isn't hanging about, reminding me that I've been rejected.

The other thing I do is write as many stories as I can.

I have at least twenty stories circulating at various times ( I used to have up to fifty when there were more markets available). Now when one or two come back, I still have at least eighteen more 'out there'.

So if having a story rejected bothers you, why not try writing dozens more? The more you write, the more you learn. The more stories you have under consideration, the more chances you have of selling one.

Possibly the most important thing to bear in mind that it isn't YOU that's being rejected.

It isn't YOU that isn't good enough. All that's happened is that the editor or judge didn't want your story at the time you sent it.

I have met lots of talented writers who never get rejected – they never send anything out!

Don't let this be you. Keep at it. Ask for feedback and listen to it and those rejections will soon start changing to sales.

## TO SUMMARISE

It's easy, when faced with a rejection, to think that there was something wrong with your story, and throw it away or file it in some forgotten drawer. Don't. Take another look at it and if you still think it has merit, try and find somewhere else to send it.

Finally, I'd like to pass on to you my top ten short story writing tips.

1. READ AS MANY SHORT STORIES AS YOU CAN
2. STUDY THE MARKET BEFORE SENDING ANYTHING OUT
3. CHECK THE WORD COUNT FITS THE MARKET/COMPETITION
4. HAVE A STRONG OPENING LINE
5. END THE STORY SOONER RATHER THAN LATER
6. MAKE SURE YOU KNOW WHOSE STORY IT IS YOU ARE TELLING
7. IF POSSIBLE, LINK THE END AND THE BEGINNING
8. READ STORIES OUT LOUD BEFORE SUBMITTING THEM
9. PROOF READ WITH CARE

and most importantly of all

10. KEEP TRYING AND NEVER GIVE UP.

Now for one final thought.

Whenever you read one of my stories in My Weekly, Yours, or the Weekly News it's likely that it will already have been rejected by other markets.

I normally send a story to Woman's Weekly or Fiction Feast first. If they both reject it, I don't give up. I rewrite the story and send it to the next market or competition on the list.

That's just one of the ways to turn a rejection into a sale!